AF580004

Dedicated to my Little Man:
"First decide what you would be, then do what you have to."
Epictetus

Hallöchen, and welcome to my international class
G'day
Namaste
Hej
Marhab

Jambo
Hey ya'll
Ciao
Olá
Ya-ho

Today we share our hopes and dreams,
so your fantasies you must show.
To set a good example,
I had better have first go.

Guten tag, I am Whilhelmina Winkler
from Germany

I will be a teacher,
I will grow the young mind.
Filling them with hope and dreams,
With all the joy they can find.

Hello, I am Jemima from England.
I will be a pilot,
flying on a cloud.
Keeping everyone safe and well,
my parents will be so proud.

G'day, I am Byron from Australia

I will be a spaceman,
I will float among the stars.
Hop into my rocket ship,
and fly all the way to Mars

Crikey!!!

Rock 'n'
Ain't noise pollution!!!

Namaste, I am Krisha from India

I will be a rock star,
I will smash my best guitar.
My mum is not quite convinced,
She wants me to play the sitar.

WOW

Hej, I am Felix from Denmark

I will be an ocean sailor,
Crossing the seven seas.
Visiting distant exciting lands,
Using nothing but the breeze.

Ciao, I am Francesca from Italy.

I will be a ballerina,
twirling way up high.
I will leap so far,
people will think I can fly.

What fantastic dreams you have,
I love to see you grow❤️
We have finished our first five,
now it is Jordon's turn to glow.

Howdy, I am Jordon from the USA

I will be a deep sea diver,
swimming with all the fish.
Maybe I will see a mermaid,
that is my greatest wish.

Ola, I am Marcia from Brazil.

I will be a movie star,
I will dazzle on the screen.
Making lots of scary movies,
listening to everyone scream.

Marhaba, I am Fahad from Oman

I will be a race car driver,
zooming around the track.
I will drive so fast,
you will only see my back.

Konichiwa, I am Niko from Japan

I will be an Olympian,
although my sports clue is zero.
I will still win a gold medal,
and be a national hero.

Jambo, I am Okello from Kenya

I will be a wizard,
taking spells from my book.
Looking for magical potions,
in the pages that I can cook.

What a fantastic day,
your dreams make me rejoice!
Such wonderful futures I can see,
as you shared your perfect choice.

To prepare for our next lesson,
you will need to think a bit.
Tell us about your country,
what really makes it a hit.

Hooroo
Bye
Kwaheri
Sayōnara
Adeus

Auf Wiedersehen,
Until the next class
my sweets🥰
Hej hej
Arrivederci
Bye
Namaskar

www.ingramcontent.com/pod-product-compliance
Lightning Source LLC
LaVergne TN
LVHW071218160826
845679LV00003B/871

* 9 7 9 8 3 6 6 9 6 6 8 1 8 *